Learn With Animals

Shapes in Animals

By
Sebastiano Ranchetti

Reading consultant: Susan Nations, M.Ed.,
author/literacy coach/consultant
in literacy development

WEEKLY READER®
PUBLISHING

circle

3

4

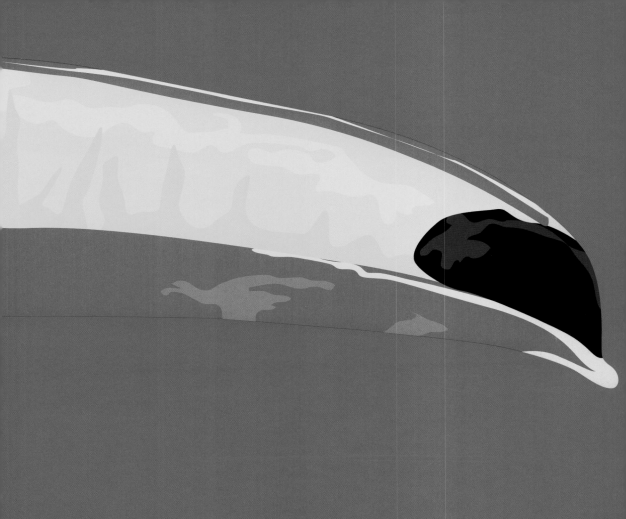

square

7

8

9

10

triangle

13

spiral

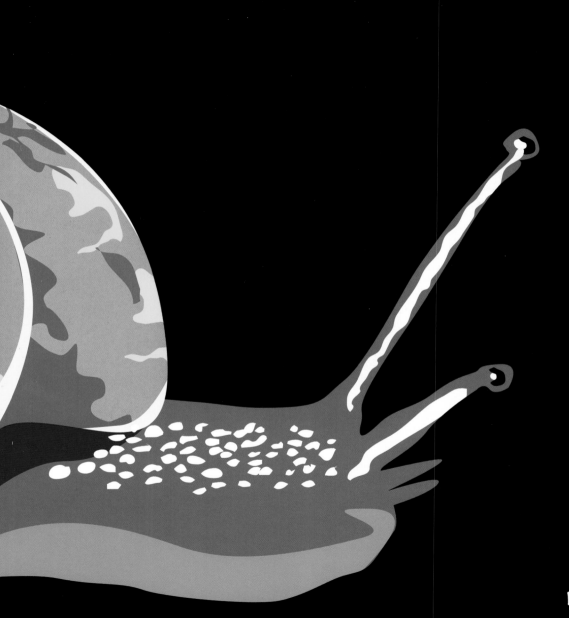

17

star

19

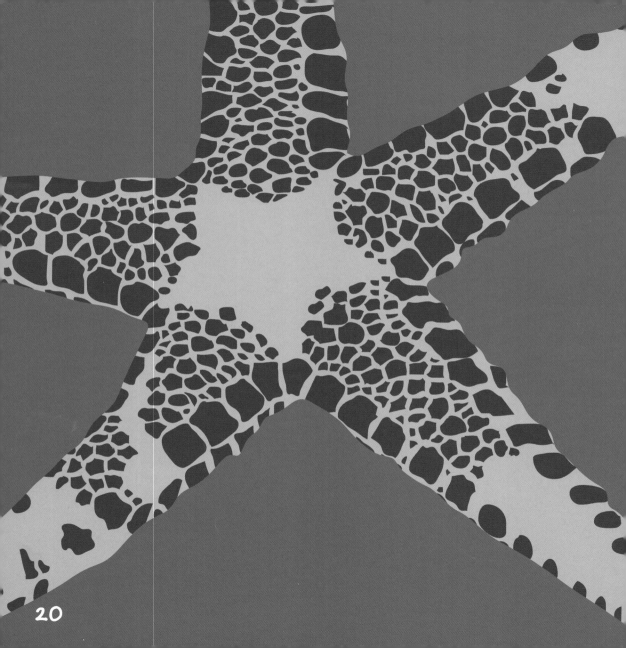

20

21

circle

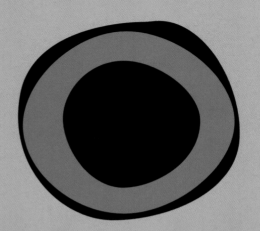

square

triangle

spiral

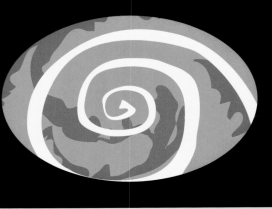

star

23

Please visit our web site at www.garethstevens.com.
For a free color catalog describing our list of high-quality books,
call 1-800-542-2595 (USA) or 1-800-387-3178 (Canada). Our fax: 877-542-2596

Library of Congress Cataloging-in-Publication Data

Ranchetti, Sebastiano.
　　　[Forme e animali. English]
　　　Shapes in animals / by Sebastiano Ranchetti—North American ed.
　　　　　p. cm.—(Learn with animals)
　　　ISBN-10: 0-8368-8824-3　ISBN-13: 978-0-8368-8824-9 (lib. bdg.)
　　　ISBN-10: 0-8368-8829-4　ISBN-13: 978-0-8368-8829-4 (softcover)
　　　1. Shapes—Juvenile literature. 2. Animals—Juvenile literature. I. Title
　　QA445.5.R36513　2008
　　516'.15—dc22　　　　　　　　　　　　　　　　　　　2007029974

This North American edition first published in 2008 by
Weekly Reader® Books
An Imprint of Gareth Stevens Publishing
1 Reader's Digest Road
Pleasantville, NY 10570-7000　USA

Gareth Stevens Senior Managing Editor: Lisa M. Guidone
Gareth Stevens Senior Editor: Barbara Bakowski
Gareth Stevens Creative Director: Lisa Donovan
Gareth Stevens Graphic Designer: Alexandria Davis

Printed in the United States of America

1 2 3 4 5 6 7 8 9 10 09 08 07

About the AUTHOR and ARTIST

SEBASTIANO RANCHETTI has illustrated many books. He lives in the countryside near Florence, Italy. His wife, three daughters, and some lively cats and dogs share his home. The ideas for his colorful drawings come from nature and animals. He hopes his books spark your imagination! Find out more at **www.animalsincolor.com**.